FREE
KICK

Also by Michael Hardcastle

Away From Home

Half a Team

In the Net

The Price of Football

Soccer Special

Team Mascot

The Team That Wouldn't Give In

United!

for younger readers

Carole's Camel

Soccer Star

Walking the Goldfish

Winning Goal

Michael Hardcastle regularly visits schools and libraries around the country. If you would like to meet him, please ask your teacher or librarian to write to the address below:

MAMMOTH Press Office
Michelin House, 81 Fulham Road, London SW3 6RB

FREE
KICK

mammoth

First published in Great Britain 1974
by Methuen Children's Books Ltd
Published 1979 by Magnet
Published 1989 by Mammoth
Reissued 1998 by Mammoth
an imprint of Reed International Books Limited
Michelin House, 81 Fulham Road, London SW3 6RB

ISBN 0 7497 0127 7

10 9 8 7 6 5 4 3 2 1

A CIP catalogue record for this title
is available from the British Library

Printed and bound in Great Britain
by Cox & Wyman Ltd, Reading, Berkshire

One

Nick Abel-Smith hobbled across the pitch to take up his position for the free kick. If it went according to plan, the ball would be played back to Ben Fairfield—and Ben would chip it into the penalty area for Nick to run on to and try a shot. Trevor Shipway, the captain, was taking the kick himself. Nick saw him glance in his direction before hitting the ball hard into the defensive wall.

That wasn't what they'd planned in training and Nick frowned. He had been given no chance at all of going for goal. The ball rebounded from the wall and Ben Fairfield, who'd been following up, wasn't able to find a gap. He tried to take on two defenders at once and, not surprisingly, lost the ball to the opposition.

Nick turned away in disgust. His team, Oakland Rangers, were a goal down with only fifteen minutes to play in this Sunday Junior League match with Alkerstone United. That goal was scored just before half-time and since then United had been hanging on to their lead like a team who know they'll be relegated if they fail to win. In fact, the season wasn't half over yet and Alkerstone, who were in the middle of the League table, had no worries about their position.

In Nick's opinion, Rangers, who were fourth from the the top, should have been winning easily. Part of the trouble, he knew, was his own injury. When his play was restricted the team's performance was bound to suffer.

But there was more to it than that. Trevor Shipway was not showing the powers of leadership that Nick expected to find in a captain. For one thing, his usual enthusiasm seemed to have disappeared. When a team is one-down a captain should be doing all he can to encourage his players. Trevor Shipway was playing at half-speed—and he was perfectly fit. Nick was furious with him.

Now, as the ball came towards him from a faulty clearance, Nick tried to sprint to reach it. The pain in his thigh was getting worse but it was bearable; it had to be, because the match wasn't over yet. Nick reached the ball a

6

split-second ahead of an opponent. The United player continued his charge and Nick avoided a collision only by twisting round on his heel. That sent another pain shooting through his leg, but he ignored it. He flicked the ball ahead of him with his other foot and jogged towards the penalty area.

He was prepared to take on all the defenders who came at him but he needed some support. Trevor was supposed to be his inside partner and co-striker but he was on the other side of the pitch, just ambling forward with no sense of urgency. Nick frowned, dummied his way past a full-back, swerved round the centre-half—and then was knocked over by a ferocious tackle from behind. The culprit was the first player he'd beaten on his run; the referee blew for a foul and then sternly lectured the offender.

Nick hauled himself to his feet and tried to flex his leg. There was a pain now in his knee and he could hardly walk. Trevor Shipway strolled up and raised his eyebrows.

"You okay, Nick?" he inquired casually.

"Just fine," Nick snapped back. "How about you?"

Trevor looked surprised. He couldn't think of

7

any reason why Nick should be in such a foul
mood.

"I'm fine, too," he answered. It seemed the best
thing to say in the circumstances. In any case, it
was the truth.

But Nick was no longer in ear-shot. He'd
limped off to where the action was—or where
he thought it would soon take place. Trevor was
the first to recognize Nick's keenness in a match
but he sometimes wondered how much of that
enthusiasm was due solely to Nick's desire to get
the ball for himself and score goals. It was

something he would have to think about again in the next few days.

The minutes were filtering away like grains of sand in an egg-timer and still Oakland couldn't get the ball into the net. Nick was reduced to a jog-trot but he was still striving to win the match for his team. The one advantage he had now was that Alkerstone believed he was as good as finished for this match. They had no doubt at all that he was severely injured and thus no threat to them. That was a bad mistake on their part. Nick would never give in as long as he was still on his feet.

Suddenly, Derek Bell, Oakland's left-half and a real dynamo in midfield, burst out of a ruck of players with the ball at his feet. He always enjoyed making a solo run for goal and there were times when he and Nick had combined brilliantly to outwit the opposition.

Bell—who was called Dinger by just about everyone—would steam up the middle with Nick acting as decoy on the left or the right. Opponents who knew of Nick's scoring record would always expect the ball to be passed to him before long. So they watched him like a fox eyes its next meal.

Meanwhile, Dinger would be thundering on alone. Often enough he would get within shooting range before laying off the ball to someone else—though not usually to Nick Abel-Smith. It was from that 'someone else' that Nick would receive the ball: a quick chip from the left or the right for Nick to run on to before turning the ball back to Dinger who would now be unmarked. And Dinger had scored many goals from that crafty move.

This time it was Nick who was unmarked: Alkerstone were still ignoring him. Even when Nick yelled for the ball from the left wing position the defenders were not worried. They didn't expect Dinger to waste an opening by passing to his crippled inside-right. Even Dinger himself seemed to hesitate—but then, remembering some of his team-mate's remarkable scoring feats, he obeyed his instincts and hit a well-judged pass in his direction.

Nick limped in to meet it. It was a luxury for him to have so much space in which to move with no defenders harrying him. He pushed the ball ahead of him as he made for the edge of the penalty area. One United player came at him fairly half-heartedly because he was expecting

Nick to get rid of the ball quickly, but Nick easily fooled him by pushing the ball past him on one side and running round to collect it on the other. Nick had no intention of losing possession yet.

He was glad that Dinger had had the good sense to stay in the middle. If he'd moved towards Nick he'd have brought a swarm of defenders with him.

Rangers' forwards were now massing in the box in anticipation of a high centre from their inside-right. Scott Hooston, their tall right-winger, had come into position himself near the upright so that he could flick the ball across the face of the goal for his captain or Ben Fairfield to apply the finishing touches.

But Nick was still not ready to part with the ball. He had noted that Scott was being closely marked by the tallest of the United defenders. At last the danger of allowing Nick so much freedom was realized by Alkerstone's skipper. He himself darted out to tackle him.

Nick defeated that aim by dragging the ball away with his left foot and then shielding it with his body as he shuffled towards the dead-ball line. Another defender came out to block the route to goal but his commonsense told him to stand-off to see what Nick would try next.

The Rangers attacker seemed scarcely to be moving at all but by now he was almost on the line. The Alkerstone captain decided on a clever move. He would rush in, kick the ball against Nick's legs so that it would rebound over the line and put an end to this attack.

Nick had guessed what was coming. As the would-be tackler rushed forward, Nick stepped back one pace, turned towards the wing—and then with his right foot savagely back-heeled the ball into the penalty area.

It took all the defenders—and some of the attackers as well—completely by surprise.

Dinger Bell swung at the ball and missed it by almost a metre; Ben Fairfield stabbed at it—and merely succeeded in deflecting it fractionally from its course; and then, with perfect coolness, Trevor Shipway stepped forward two paces and hit it into the net just inside the far upright while the United goalkeeper stood as motionless as a deep frozen fish.

That equalizer was greeted with enormous relief and enthusiasm by every member of the Oakland team—with the exception of the player who'd created the opening, Nick Abel-Smith. He was making his way slowly back to the centre with no expression at all on his thin face or in his dark eyes. However, he deigned to acknowledge with a flick of his hand Trevor's congratulatory wave. Nick simply felt that he had accomplished what he'd intended and now it was time to get on with the game and score the winning goal. Two points were at stake in this match, not one, as he would have pointed out if he'd been the captain.

Still, it was noticeable now that Shipway was showing some eagerness to repeat his feat. In the manner of most teams when they've just conceded a goal, Alkerstone rushed forward frantically from the kick-off in the hope of restoring their lead. Their centre-forward displayed some neat footwork as he rounded the Rangers' centre-half before hitting the ball into space on the right.

Dinger Bell had to spin round and dash after it and he had just enough speed to catch up with it first in a race with United's right-winger. He hit a square pass to his left-back, who wasted no time in blasting the ball back down the middle.

Scott Hooston had shown intelligence in coming inside and it was he who headed the ball on to Nick. The Rangers inside-right gave the impression that he was going to keep possession again because, after trapping the ball, he rolled it back and forth under his boot. But when a United player rushed at him, Nick flicked the ball sideways towards his captain.

Trevor Shipway was already on the move. With the United defence still out of position following their surge upfield from the kick-off he had only two opponents between himself and the goal. He quickened his pace very effectively to beat one of them and when the second came in to challenge, Trevor slipped the ball sideways to Ben Fairfield, who was right on the edge of the penalty area.

Ben, who believed in shooting on sight, simply hit the ball with all the power he possessed. From that range he would have been lucky to put the ball past a reasonably agile goalkeeper. As it was, the United goalie simply stuck out a hand and by sheer luck diverted the ball on to the crossbar. But there was enough force in Ben's shot for the ball to bounce almost straight back across the penalty area.

From thé moment he had retrieved the ball and passed it to his full-back, Dinger Bell hadn't stopped running. Now he was haring into the penalty area as the ball came towards him. Dinger slowed down, steadied himself, allowed the ball to bounce just once more—and then, with remarkably good aim, drove it past the stranded goalkeeper into the bottom corner of the net.

Dinger was overjoyed and so was Ben Fairfield, who believed that he had done just as much as the left-half in setting up the goal. Trevor Shipway praised them both and modestly accepted their congratulations on his part in the movement that had led to Rangers taking the lead. Even Nick managed to look quite pleased for once. For it now seemed certain that Rangers were going to collect two points after all.

Alkerstone were thoroughly dismayed. especially when, a few moments later, the referee brought the match to an end with a long blast of his whistle and a furious waving of his arms.

Though the players didn't know it at that moment, Rangers had moved one more place up the League table into third position. They were ready now to challenge the leaders, Merrywood Colts.

As the teams trudged off the pitch to the dressing-rooms Trevor Shipway dropped back to see whether Nick needed a helping hand. Nick said he could manage very well on his own, though he was now limping heavily. He felt quite drained of energy whereas he was usually feeling on top of the world after his side had won an important match.

"That was a great result," Trevor remarked. "I didn't think we were going to make it until I got the equalizer."

"We left it a bit late. I thought you'd just about given up hope," Nick told him. He didn't think that Trevor ought to claim much credit for scoring the first goal.

Trevor didn't rise to that bait. His mind seemed to be on something else. He was silent for a few moments—and then made an announcement that took Nick completely by surprise. That was exactly what Trevor had intended to do.

"Well," he said, taking his time over every word, "I hope we can keep on winning like this until I finish. I'd like Rangers to be on top of the League when I leave."

Nick had stopped dead in his tracks. "Finish?" he said, baffled. "What are you talking about?"

Two other members of the team, Scott Hooston and Dinger Bell, had overheard the conversation and they, too, halted. They were just as interested as Nick in hearing what Trevor was going to say next.

Trevor, aware of how much attention he'd aroused, now adopted a very casual attitude. "Oh, we're moving at the end of the month— didn't you know? My Dad's got a new job in London, so we're going to live there. I expect there'll be plenty of London teams that'll want me to play for them."

Nick had listened to every word but his mind had seized on only one fact. Oakland Rangers were going to need a new captain. In Nick's opinion, there was only one possible choice: himself.

"Well, in that case, Trevor," he said blandly, "I shall have to take over from you as captain. I mean, there's no one—"

"Oh, no you don't!" Dinger Bell cut in. "I'm the best one to be the new captain."

"Rubbish!" Scott Hooston shouted. "I'm going to be captain!"

Two

By the time they reached the dressing-room the three candidates for the captaincy were arguing so fiercely among themselves that Trevor Shipway had to assert his authority to calm them down. He said that if there was any more squabbling none of them would be picked for the next match. He knew that he wouldn't be able to carry out such a threat, because the team needed each of them, but at least it shut them up for the moment.

Dinger Bell was the first to recover. "Well," he said, "we shall have to vote on it, shan't we? I mean, that's the fairest way. Right, who's going to vote for me for captain? Put your hands—"

"Oh, no!" Nick interrupted him sharply. He knew that although he was the best player in the team he wasn't popular enough with his team-mates to get enough votes in a contest like this.

18

So there had to be another way of picking the captain. "I'm the only one here who's played for the town junior team, Town Boys. That's like getting a cap for England. So the captain has to be the best player in the team. That's logical."

"No, it's not," Scott countered. "The captain of England isn't always the best player. He's the one chosen by the Manager."

"We haven't got a Manager," Nick pointed out triumphantly.

"Then Trevor should pick the next captain," Dinger said, knowing that his friendship with Trevor should count heavily in his favour. "How about it, Trevor? I mean, it seems fair that the present captain should choose the one to follow him."

But that idea didn't appeal to Scott, either. There were times when Trevor had left him out of the team and played Rupert Mitchell in his place. So he knew that Shipway didn't regard him as one of the best players—or even as a regular member of the team. Scott was constantly trying to prove to everyone that he was as good as any-one else.

"If Trevor's leaving the team it won't matter to him who the next captain is," Scott tried to

19

explain. "It's up to the rest of us to make up our own minds."

While he was talking he was attempting to work out who could be counted on to vote for him. It was rather worrying that he could think of only two, at most.

"Well," Trevor said quietly as several of the players turned to him to see what he had to say in reply to Scott's remark, "I really don't mind how the next captain is chosen. But a captain has an important job to do, you know. He has to lead the team properly—he has to *inspire* the other players...."

"*Exactly*," Nick cut in, sarcastically. Then when Trevor failed to respond, he added: "And it's always the best, the cleverest player, who provides the inspiration. So—"

"Well, who says *you're* the best player?" Dinger asked. "Just because you played for Town Boys *months* ago doesn't mean you're the best player now. You weren't so brilliant today—or last week—or the week before that—or—"

"I happen to have been injured, that's why I haven't been scoring as many goals as usual," Nick retaliated quickly. "But you wouldn't notice that, Bell. You only think about yourself, and how you're playing. And don't forget that I got my injury playing for Town Boys, when I had to take over as goalkeeper to save the team from defeat. That's what a good captain should do—be prepared to play anywhere for the sake of the team!"

There was a note of triumph in his voice as he said that; he knew it was a very convincing argument. It had probably won him one or two more supporters. So perhaps it wouldn't be such a bad idea after all to have a vote.

It was obvious now to Trevor that the problem of picking the next captain wasn't going to be solved easily. He knew very well that Nick *was* the best player in the Rangers team; but Nick was too outspoken about other boys' failings when they didn't play well. Instead of encouraging his players Nick, as captain, might well cause them to play worse.

Dinger, on the other hand, was too selfish. He was only interested in what *he* was doing and what he thought he could do. The only reason he had just criticized Nick was that he hadn't been getting many passes from him. Dinger sometimes tried *too* hard; and, as a result, he exhausted himself long before a match was over.

Trevor knew that it was important for a captain to be popular with his players. If they didn't like their captain a team wouldn't respond to his leadership. He himself wouldn't wish to play under the captaincy of either Nick or Dinger. But who else was suited to the job? It had been a surprise to him that Scott Hooston fancied himself as skipper. Were there others who also wanted to lead Rangers?

"Well," he said, choosing his words carefully, "we don't want to start any fights about the captaincy. So I think we ought to find out what everybody thinks about this. First, is there anybody else who would like to be captain? Apart from Nick, Dinger and Scott, I mean."

"Yes," Ben Fairfield said immediately. "Me."

"And me," Rupert Mitchell echoed.

Nick was about to raise some objection to that rather unexpected declaration but Trevor had sensed it was coming and he raised his hand to quell any comments.

"Okay," he said. "Fine. That's five who want to be captain. Now—"

"Hang on," a voice said. "I'd like to have a go as well. If every other forward in the team wants to be captain then I'm not going to be left out."

The speaker was James Fagan, the quietest member of the team. He played on the left wing where, from time to time, he displayed some quite astonishing footwork. In spite of being small, he had a very good turn of speed on a dry pitch. In mud, however, he was hopeless.

James was a shy boy and said very little. He always signed his name Jas. Fagan (because his grandfather had done so) and somebody had started to call him Jazz. The name had stuck and now he was Jazz to everybody.

Trevor tried not to show any surprise. It had already occurred to him that with no fewer than six volunteers for the captaincy a voting system would be of no use at all. It was unlikely that any candidate could now be the winner—the outright winner, anyway—on a show of hands. If each one voted for himself there would only be six players left, including himself, to vote for the six would-be captains. And that was a ridiculous situation.

It was Carl Beckingham, the centre-half and a newcomer to the team, who came up with the brightest suggestion.

"I think those who want to be captain should prove that they're good enough for the job," he said. "So why don't we have a competition with all of them taking part? Then the winner would take over as the new captain."

"Hey, that's a great idea," Trevor agreed. He wished he'd thought of it himself. "We could have all sorts of contests and give points for first, second and third."

"You mean a Superstar Contest," Carl added, determined not to have his brainwave snatched away from him and claimed by someone else. "The first bit of it could be a race—a 100-metre sprint to show who's the fittest candidate. And the fastest runner, of course."

"And penalty kicks," Trevor said. "That would prove who had the coolest nerves in the moment of truth."

"And a climbing race as well," someone else suggested. "That's a real test of nerves. We could have them all climbing up that sheer face of the old quarry at Cricket Hill."

"What, all together?" Trevor asked.

"Oh no," he was told. "Each boy could go up on his own and we'd time them to see who got to the top in the fastest time."

By now the rest of the team had entered into the spirit of the idea and suggestions flowed in like water into a reservoir. Boxing, wrestling, archery, darts, chess, swimming, cross-country running, weight-lifting: the list might have gone on for ever if Trevor Shipway hadn't called a halt.

"Look," he said, "this Superstar Contest is going to need a lot of working out. We can't decide everything now. So what we'll do is this: we'll have a committee of judges to arrange everything. I'll be the chairman and chief judge—that's only fair because I'm still captain of Rangers. But I want to pick a couple of helpers. If nobody objects, I'll have Carl Beckingham and Jackie Allerton. Carl because the Superstar Contest was his idea and Jackie because he's been with the team longer than anyone. Okay? Any objections?"

Only Nick had one. "The other two judges are both defenders. That's not a good idea. They can't judge how good forwards are."

Trevor had the answer to that. "Well, they've got to be defenders," he pointed out crushingly. "All the forwards want to be the next captain."

That drew a laugh from everyone except Nick and his fellow attackers. Nick, however, didn't really mind. He himself thought the contest was a good idea.

"Right, then," Trevor said with the finality he felt every captain should display when making a vital decision, "you can leave it to the three of us to sort things out this evening. We'll announce the details of the contest when we all meet for our weekly training session on Tuesday night."

The Superstar Contest Committee, under the chairmanship of Trevor Richard Shipway, did their work well and kept their promise to reveal their findings the following Tuesday. They had considered a great many possibilities for the various events but they believed that the five they had chosen were the best for the purpose of the Contest.

As Trevor explained to his assembled team-mates, each event had been selected because it would test a certain quality in the candidates. He was particularly pleased that he had managed to bring a touch of alliteration to the task.

The qualities were: speed, stamina, skill, strength and soccer sense.

The Contest would be decided, he continued, on a points basis. The winner of each single event would be awarded five points; the runner-up

28

would receive three points; and the third, one point. If any candidate was unable, for any reason, to take part in any of the events that was just hard lines. The Contest had to be completed in three weeks because that was as long as he could remain captain himself. So there could be no extension of time for illness or accidents or anything like that.

The three judges, Trevor said, would attend every event and their decision was to be final; there was to be no arguing by any of the contestants with the judges' verdict. For their part, they would do everything in their power to be completely fair to everyone.

He knew that every member of the team who wasn't competing for the captaincy would want to watch the various events but he didn't think it would be a good thing for them to take sides. If that happened, he explained, some of the candidates might not have any personal supporters and that could affect their personal performances.

"Probably make 'em try all the harder," Nick muttered, but Trevor ignored that remark.

"Okay," he said, "now to the events themselves. When we'd decided what they were going to be we then had to decide on the order in which they'd take place. That wasn't at all easy, so we actually had a raffle. We—"

"You mean a draw, Trevor," Carl interjected.

"—a draw, then," Trevor acknowledged. "And this is the order:

"First, a race over 200 metres;

"Second, a swimming race over three lengths of the Town Baths—we did check, by the way, that you can all swim;

"Third, a rifle-shooting competition—I'll give you more details of that in a minute;

"Fourth, the fastest climb up the old quarry at Cricket Hill;

"And, last, a penalty kick competition with each candidate having five shots.

"And that's it, lads."

Each candidate reacted in his own way but all of them were temporarily speechless as they worked out the implications of the events that had been chosen to test their fitness for the captaincy.

Nick's first thought was that it was rotten bad luck that the 200-metre race should be the first event of all. It was bound to be held during the next few days and he doubted that his groin injury would have healed properly by then. It had

30

been bothering him, on and off, for weeks and the knocks he'd received in Sunday's match had certainly aggravated it. The rifle-shooting competition was the real surprise, but it sounded interesting. Nick had never fired a gun of any sort in his life but he didn't suppose any of the other candidates had, either.

Dinger was the first to ask about it. Where was this shoot-in going to take place and who was providing the rifles?

"Ah, I thought you'd want to know a bit more about that," Trevor said with a satisfied air. "But I think I'd better let Jackie explain about it because it was his idea. And a good one, in my opinion—and Carl's, too."

Jackie Allerton was the team's goalkeeper. He'd been picked for that position originally because of his size, for he was built on the lines of a professional wrestler.

But Jackie had proved he had the ability to do the job well; he was surprisingly quick on his feet and he could catch the ball like an England cricket captain fielding at first slip. Like Jazz Fagan, he didn't say much and he revealed very little about himself. He turned up for the Sunday League matches and training sessions but, mainly because he attended a school none of the other players went to, his team-mates knew very little about him.

"My Dad's a champion shot with the rifle," he told them now. "He's a member of a Club which has its own shooting range and he keeps suggesting I go along there with him to learn to shoot myself."

He paused as he realized how badly he had expressed that—and his listeners enjoyed the joke. But their laughter soon died away when Jackie continued. After all, they were keen to hear more about the shooting competition.

"I mean, he wants me to learn to shoot. I've been down a couple of times and it's really very interesting. Anyway, he said I could invite a pal if I wanted to, so that we could shoot against each other. They use point-22 rifles and shoot at targets at a distance of twenty metres, or something like that.

"Well, I thought all those who want to be captain could go along and have a competition. I'm sure my Dad would fix it up for us. It would prove how good your eyesight is, and your aim, and the steadiness of your hand—and, well, all sorts of things. It's great, really, is shooting. I think I might be an Army marksman when I'm a bit older."

Trevor was nodding vigorously. "Yes, as Jackie was saying, a rifle-shooting competition will test a lot of skills all at once. So that's why we've included it."

Scott Hooston wanted to know whether they'd have a chance to practise first. But Trevor, supported by his fellow judges, said it would be fairer if they just went for the competition because it might not be possible for everyone to get along for practice at the same time. In any case, Mr Allerton might not be able to arrange more than one visit to the range for them during the next three weeks.

Ben Fairfield seemed more interested in the quarry climb than anything else and said he thought that ought to be first. He didn't tell them that he'd done a lot of rock climbing and that he believed he could win this event and so have a flying start in the contest for the captaincy. But that was what he was thinking.

However, Trevor Shipway and his fellow judges refused to consider changing the order of events. The draw had been a fair one, he assured them again, so there was no point in having another one or altering the order of play.

Patiently he dealt with a few more queries but the only important one concerned the date for the first event. "Oh yes," he said, "sorry I forgot to mention that. The 200-metre sprint will take place at 11 o'clock on Saturday morning on the Common.

"Right, now let's get down to some serious football training. We've got an important match with Bank Vale United on Sunday."

Three

When Nick Abel-Smith awoke on Saturday morning his first thought was about the weather—and his second thought was about his thigh injury. He got out of bed very carefully and tested his right leg before daring to put his full weight on it. To his great relief, there was hardly any ache at all, just the merest twinge of pain. That was a very hopeful sign for earlier in the week he'd still been limping. So the heat treatment he'd been given the previous evening must have done him a lot of good.

That treatment had been provided by the physiotherapist who was on the staff of Albion Football Club, the local First Division side. Nick was one of the schoolboys they took a close interest in with an eye to the future and so he was welcome to visit the Club from time to time. He had met the physiotherapist, Mr Fallon, on

one occasion and, when school was over on Friday afternoon, he had gone to Albion's treatment room to ask for help.

Gently but thoroughly, Mr Fallon's fingers had probed the troubled area and Nick did his best not to show any reaction. "Well," said Mr Fallon, "I'll give you a bit of a massage and then you can have a spell under the lamp. Heat treatment can sometimes be very effective with injuries like yours. But I'm not giving you any pills, that's for sure, If the pain starts up again you'll either have to grin and bear it or pack up what you're doing. Pain is a warning, you know —a warning that something is wrong somewhere. So it shouldn't be ignored."

Nick had felt a lot more relaxed after the heat treatment and the massage. Much to his parents' surprise, he had gone to bed early on the Friday evening so that he could have maximum rest before the race.

Now, as he walked cautiously across his bedroom to the window, he was wondering what the weather was like. If it was raining, and the Common was muddy, he would be delighted. For the mud would slow down all the runners—and Nick's chance of winning the race would be greatly improved. He knew he wasn't the fastest player in the team but he had hopes of finishing in the first three and so picking up at least one point.

It wasn't easy to predict the outcome of the race, he decided. Dinger Bell could go a bit but he might run out of steam over the last 50 metres. Scott Hooston was no real speed merchant in spite of his long legs (thin legs with no muscles,

Nick remembered). Jazz would be okay on hard ground but probably 200 metres was too far for him, too. Ben Fairfield wasn't a sprinter under any conditions. In fact, Rupert Mitchell might be the fastest of them all because he could certainly move when he wanted to on the football field. At other times, he was dead lazy, in Nick's opinion.

Nick reached the bedroom window and drew back the curtain. From the condensation on the pane he knew at once that there'd been a frost during the night. There hadn't been any rain for several days and it didn't look as though the dry spell was going to be broken today. A pale sun was shining already and the ground was obviously rock-hard.

It was disappointing but there was nothing he could do about it. Before getting dressed he did half-a-dozen press-ups on the bedroom floor and then went down to breakfast. His parents were about to go out shopping together so he could take his time over the meal. Mrs Abel-Smith took more interest than her husband in their only son's sporting activities but Nick hadn't mentioned the Superstar Contest to them. His mother assumed that after breakfast Nick would go out on his usual Saturday morning training run and then return in time to watch the lunch-time football programme on television.

Nick filled a cereal bowl with muesli and added some milk. The muesli was home-made from wheat flakes, oat flakes, nuts, honey, sultanas and brown sugar and Nick had once been told that it was a perfect food for sportsmen because it provided so much energy.

After making himself one piece of toast—it wasn't advisable to eat too much just before a race—and covering it with marmalade he picked up a sports magazine and read that until he'd finished breakfast. The magazine contained an article about "the art of taking a free kick" and Nick read it twice; it seemed to him to be full of useful tips and he might well be able to put them into practice when he became captain of Oakland Rangers. A captain had to be thinking about the game all the time and planning how to take advantage of corner kicks, free kicks and throw-ins.

He carried out his Saturday chore of washing up all the breakfast dishes and then he was free to go out for a spot of training to loosen up his muscles before the race. He wondered what his rivals were doing. Dinger Bell was a fitness fanatic and probably had been out training every night since Tuesday. In Nick's eyes, Dinger was the one he had to beat to win the prize.

When Nick reached the Common, where the race was to be run, Dinger was the first person he saw. In the past they'd have greeted each other warmly and chatted away for ages about soccer tactics and recent matches. Now they merely nodded at one another and then turned away to jog up and down to keep warm. Both were wearing their favourite track-suits and a few minutes earlier had been practising sprint starts.

Nick was feeling in good form. He hadn't, of course, tested himself to the full in training but his thigh was giving him no trouble at all at the moment; there wasn't even a vague feeling of discomfort.

Trevor Shipway and his fellow judges arrived together, with Trevor twirling round his index finger a starting pistol he'd borrowed from someone. He was determined that everything should be done properly in this Contest. He wasn't going to leave himself open to any complaints about the organization of the tournament.

"Feeling fit, lads?" he inquired cheerfully. Two

nods of acknowledgement was the only reply he received. But the other competitors, who arrived a few moments later, were in a more cheerful mood. All were wearing their football shorts and shirts under tracksuits so there was going to be no delay in starting the race. Quite a number of supporters had turned up to cheer on their particular friends but no one seemed to be claiming that he knew for certain who was going to win the race. Generally, it was thought to be fairly open although Dinger was probably just the favourite.

The straight track had been measured very carefully earlier in the week and checked twice since then. The ground was level except for a sharp dip just after the halfway point. As chief judge Trevor knew that he really ought to be on the finishing line but he couldn't be there and act as starter as well. Since acquiring the pistol he had decided that the job of starter was the more important because a false start could give an advantage to some competitors. In any case, he reminded himself, he had two fellow judges and they were going to be stationed on the finishing line. There had been no difficulty about persuading two boys to hold the tape: the team's fullback's, Phil Astbury and Mark Haskayne, had volunteered for the task.

"Right, then," Trevor called, "it's time to line up. We haven't been able to mark out running lanes but you'll all be expected to keep to a straight line. My two judges on the finishing line will be watching to see that there's no interference among the runners and that everything's fair. If it's a very close finish they will decide the first three places—and they can also call on Phil and Mark for their opinion if necessary.

"Oh, and one last thing, the most *important* thing of all. When the race is over there's to be no arguing about the judges' verdict. That's what judges are for—to make a final decision. So, no quarrels."

The runners removed their track-suits, did a few exercises, and then took up positions on the starting line. Nick, who'd had a good look at the track, had decided that the outside position might be the best. There didn't seem to be any bumps or hollows on that lane.

Fortunately, no one else was mad-keen to have that position but there was a minor squabble between Scott Hooston and Dinger Bell for the inside lane. That was resolved when Trevor said

42

firmly that Scott had been there first and the position was his. Dinger muttered under his breath but moved over to the second lane. Rupert Mitchell and Ben Fairfield took the middle lanes and Jazz Fagan was next to Nick.

They all crouched down on the order "Get set!" Tensed on "Steady!" And were into their stride as the pistol cracked a split-second later.

It was a remarkably even break and Trevor felt justified in congratulating himself on his timing as the runners sprinted away from him.

Dinger Bell was the first to show in front, just ahead of Rupert Mitchell and Scott Hooston. Nick felt that he was running very easily and he was more concerned about keeping some speed in reserve for the finish. He had told himself earlier that he must keep looking straight ahead but now he couldn't resist a glance to his right to see where Dinger was. He wasn't at all surprised that Bell was leading. But it was the finish that mattered.

After 50 metres Dinger had increased his advantage over Rupert but Scott was closing on both of them. Nick was in fourth place and Jazz just behind him. The only competitor who seemed to be struggling was Ben Fairfield. He was dropping further behind all the time.

By now the spectators had started to cheer on their favourites and Dinger's fan club was making a lot of noise.

That support encouraged Dinger to try and increase his speed. He accelerated and opened up a sizeable gap. Scott now daren't delay his challenge and he, too, surged forward, overtaking Rupert as he did so.

Nick, also, thought it was time he put on a spurt and within a few strides the leading quartet had pulled well ahead of the others. Jazz appeared

merely to be cruising along but Ben was surely out of the race now.

Scott was just on the point of overhauling Dinger when they reached the dip in the ground. He tried to accelerate, but the uneven ground was against him. And next moment Scott stumbled—and then fell, full length. Fortunately for Dinger, his rival didn't land in his path. Dinger was not impeded at all.

At the same moment that Scott was falling, Nick, who was still stepping up his pace, felt a sharp pain in his thigh. Automatically, he slowed up. He was sure he'd pulled a muscle or that his

45

old injury was complaining in its own way about all this extra exertion. Yet, in a few strides, the pain had gone as quickly as it had come. Nick felt it was worth the risk to change gear again and try and catch the leaders.

In the interval, however, Jazz Fagan had swept past him and was now in hot pursuit of the two leaders, Dinger Bell and Rupert Mitchell. The race was now three-quarters over and Dinger was in front by a clear stride. He intended to stay there.

But Rupert wasn't giving in. He was battling along for all he was worth. Both boys were certain that the race now lay between them. They were completely unaware of the rapid progress being made by Jazz Fagan.

The little left-winger had been running easily so far without using up any great amount of energy. He had worked out earlier in the week that his best chance of victory was in conserving himself for a late run. He knew that his burst of speed over a short distance could prove decisive— on firm ground. And his luck was in, for the turf of the Common felt as firm as concrete.

Dinger was at last beginning to weaken. He could see the finishing line getting nearer all the time, but suddenly it seemed to be taking much longer to get there. Rupert drew level with him and Dinger put his head down and summoned up all his resources for a final effort.

Yet, in the very moment that Dinger pulled ahead of Rupert once more, Jazz Fagan flashed past him as if the race for him had only just begun. Dinger could hardly believe it—and by the time he did, Jazz was across the finishing line and taking the tape with him. He was the clear winner of the first event in the Oakland Rangers Superstar Contest.

Dinger just managed to hold on to second place from Rupert Mitchell before dropping to the ground, exhausted. Nick finished in fourth place, beaten by less than a stride for a valuable point. He knew that if he hadn't slowed up he would have been right on Dinger's heels and might even have clinched second place. Ben Fairfield, having realized some time ago that his pursuit of the leaders was hopeless, didn't even bother to complete the course.

Nick immediately began a tender exploration of the zone from which the pain had emanated. He wasn't looking for, or expecting, any sympathy from the spectators or the judges or anyone else. He simply wanted to try and find out whether the trouble was likely to recur. Surprisingly, it seemed perfectly all right. No pain. No discomfort. No sensation at all. And, when he thought about it again, no points for him from the first stage of the tournament.

Meanwhile, there were congratulations for the winner. Jazz's success had surprised nearly everyone (though not the winner himself, of course). Now that he had five points to his credit his bid for the captaincy had to be taken seriously.

Jazz took his victory very modestly but was obviously pleased about it. But he knew there was a long way to go before the ultimate winner of the tournament picked his first team as captain. Still, he himself was now leading the field so far as all the candidates were concerned.

For the time being, Trevor was still captain—and he was confirming his position by making another announcement.

"Right, lads, as we're all together I think we ought to have a word about tomorrow's match, here on the Common, with Bank Vale United. It's one we've just got to win if we're going to keep up our challenge for the Championship."

Four

For part of the previous season, Nick Abel-Smith had played for Bank Vale United and it hadn't really been a very happy experience for anyone. After only a few matches with United he had moved on again and joined Oakland Rangers.

United were led by Keith Nash, their right-half, a good player but hardly a strong enough character (in Nick's opinion) to be captain. Nick had been very friendly with one of the United forwards, Kevin Ripley, and for a time Kevin had tried to arrange for Nick to take over as skipper. But Keith managed to hold on to the leadership and, disappointed by the way things had turned out, Nick left.

He knew that Keith and Kevin were firm friends again for they had been on the Town Boys' tour with Nick. Their attitude towards him had been very chilly and he expected that this afternoon's match between United and Rangers was going to contain plenty of tension. Keith, for one, would want to make certain that Nick was blotted out of the game so that he couldn't score against his old team. Nonetheless, Nick hoped there wouldn't be any ill-feeling or dirty play. He always played fairly himself but he was aware that Kevin, in particular, had some dubious tricks in his repertoire.

There'd been a moment the previous day, following the Superstar race, when Nick had feared that he wasn't even going to be playing in the match. Trevor had quietly asked him how fit he was.

"I saw you slow up in the race and thought your injury must be bothering you again," he explained. "You've had a bit of a battering lately and if you want a rest tomorrow that's okay with me, Nick. I mean, we've got Rupert Mitchell in reserve and I think he might play well tomorrow. Finishing third in this race will have given him a boost."

Nick shook his head. "No, I'm fine. The thigh strain seems to be better now. Anyway, you need me against United."

That wasn't said at all boastfully. He simply

knew exactly what his value was to the team, not only as a goal-scorer but as a tactician. Trevor didn't challenge the statement. So the matter of Nick's "rest" was dropped and not raised again. In fact, when they went on to talk about the composition of the side he accepted Nick's recommendation that Rupert should take over from Scott but play in the middle rather than on the wing.

Nick knew that he himself was going to be shadowed as closely as possible by the United defence and therefore if he operated from the wing defenders would be drawn out of position. Hopefully, that would then leave gaps down the middle for Trevor, Rupert and Ben to exploit. Trevor was quite delighted by that scheme. He enjoyed scoring goals as much as any centre-forward and he wanted to finish his days with Rangers in a blaze of glory.

The United players were already shooting-in at the far goal when Trevor and his team arrived at the pitch on the Common. The Rangers captain didn't believe in rushing anything when it wasn't necessary and he told his boys to take their time over changing. In fact, all that was required for most of them was to strip off their track-suits.

They were already wearing their all-red outfit underneath.

United were lying in fifth position in the Sunday League table and lately they'd had a very good run by winning four out of five matches. They knew that Rangers would be tough opposition but they were doubly keen to beat them simply because Nick Abel-Smith was in their ranks. Keith and Kevin had devised a plan to subdue their former team-mate and they were reasonably confident that it would work, although they recognized Nick's brilliance both in creating chances to score—and taking them.

Trevor won the toss and decided to kick-off because he was keen to attack from the start. Nick was in the middle with him but as soon as the ball was in motion he changed places with Rupert Mitchell who preferred to act as a striker in the middle anyway. Nick had guessed correctly that Keith Nash himself would move into the middle "to put the shackles on him", in a sports-writer's phrase. But Keith was plainly worried by Nick's move out to the right flank. He was naturally a right-footed player and so he wasn't going to find it easy to control the game from the left—and keep Nick quiet at the same time.

There was little enough time for Keith to put another plan into operation for Rangers were already in full cry. Inspired, perhaps, by his sprinting success the previous day, Jazz Fagan was displaying some dazzling footwork on the opposite flank. Twice he sent the United full-back the wrong way before hitting the ball into the middle.

Rupert Mitchell, who was determined to keep his place in the team after this match, won his race with the United centre-half for the ball and then cleverly turned it to the left again. Jazz hadn't stopped running (ever since Saturday's race he'd been wondering whether he might not reach Olympic standards as a runner one day) and from the edge of the box he chipped the ball towards the near post. It really was a very shrewd move, for Trevor Shipway had cut inside and was there to head the ball across the face of the goal.

With Keith still out on the other wing and his left-half stranded in midfield where he'd been attempting to cover for his captain, the United defenders were woefully out of position. So they had only themselves to blame when Dinger Bell came scorching up the middle as if trying to prove

53

that his defeat the previous day had been due solely to bad luck. Ben Fairfield, who had taken over Nick's role, pulled the ball down well from Trevor's headed centre. He stepped back two paces to baffle an opponent and then slipped the ball sideways for the in-rushing Dinger.

And Dinger hit it with rare force and accuracy. The ball went crashing into the roof of the net almost before the United goalkeeper could move.

It was such a good goal, and so well taken, that Nick had no hesitation in calling out his congratulations to Dinger. The left-half was so overjoyed with his feat that he even responded with a wave of his hand in Nick's direction before he was submerged by his ecstatic colleagues.

For United, it was a stupefying situation. They had been so certain that the main threat would come from Nick Abel-Smith—and Nick had contributed nothing to the game so far. At least, nothing positive; it was merely his presence on the field that had affected them and their play.

Nick was amused to see a very animated conversation taking place between Keith Nash and Edward Lancaster, United's left-half, the boy who really ought to have had the job of marking Nick from the outset. Edward, red-haired, freckled and

54

very strong, was a tough tackler and perfectly capable of looking after any opposing forward. He had joined United during Nick's spell with the team and he became a great admirer of the free-scoring striker.

All the same, now that Nick was playing for another team, Edward would be just as determined to shut him out of the game for United's sake. His captain, however, had decided that he himself was the one best equipped to deal with Abel-Smith. Edward had accepted that arrangement without question—but now, following Rangers' goal, he wasn't surprised to be told that Keith had changed his mind. For the rest of the game, Edward was to ensure that Abel-Smith remained as harmless as a toothless lap-dog.

It didn't matter to Nick what plans had been made to restrict his play so long as *somebody* on the United side stayed out on the wing with him; for that meant that there was one defender fewer for his team-mates to contend with in the middle. Rangers were still dominating the game and Jazz Fagan was having a great time on the opposite flank.

Keith Nash seemed still to be suffering from the effects of that early goal and very little was going right for him. Even Kevin Ripley, who normally stayed up-front for any half-chance that might be turned into a goal, had dropped back to assist the beleaguered United defence. Rupert Mitchell was showing that he possessed more than mere enthusiasm and one shot on the turn from just inside the box could easily have brought Rangers their second goal.

When, at last, Nick did get a touch of the ball it was quite by accident. A faulty clearance from United's left-back drifted in Nick's direction and he sprinted to meet it. Edward Lancaster pursued him like a whippet chasing a rabbit but Nick had no intention of keeping possession—yet. He turned on the ball, flicked it against Lancaster's legs and then coolly took the throw-in himself to send Trevor Shipway off on another raid deep into United territory. Nick grinned at the look of frustration on Lancaster's face.

"Don't worry, Edward," he joked. "I'll let you see the ball next time. Won't do you much good, though. I can dribble past you whenever I want to."

Five minutes before half-time United at long last forced their way into the Rangers penalty area. Keith Nash had set up the attack with a long ball down the middle for his tall, gangling centre-forward to run on to and then beat Carl Beckingham with a very neat side-step. After such a lengthy spell without being under much pressure the Rangers defenders were rather slow to see the danger and close the gap.

Kevin Ripley wasn't—and he hurtled into the box as the centre-forward slid the ball out to the right. United's nippy right-winger, Gary Ansell, took the ball almost to the dead-ball line before lifting it back into the middle. The centre-forward jumped well and headed the ball towards the top right-hand corner of the net.

Jackie Allerton managed to get his fingers to the shot and knocked the ball down. That was just the chance Ripley had been hoping for and he jack-knifed forward in an effort to divert the ball with his head into the bottom of the net. But in the very moment that he made contact with the ball he also collided heavily with the tumbling figure of Jackie—and Jackie, in falling right on top of Kevin, flattened him almost into the shape of a pancake. Kevin was momentarily in no fit state to see where the ball went—and, anyway, he'd have been disgusted that it had bounced harmlessly over the line for a goal-kick.

United's substitute, who'd had some first-aid training, came on to minister to Kevin who, plainly, was a bit dazed—as any player of his size would have been after suffering the weight of Jackie Allerton on top of him. It was an indication of how shaken he felt that Kevin didn't even protest that the referee should have awarded a corner, not a goal-kick. A few moments later he shook off the substitute's attentions and staggered back towards the middle. But not for long.

During a skirmish in midfield the referee had a quick word with Kevin who appeared to be still feeling the effects of the steam-roller treatment he'd suffered. The boy might, the referee considered, have mild concussion so he really ought to rest for a while. "Take a break," he said to Kevin. "It's nearly half-time, so you won't miss much."

Surprisingly (to those who knew him, anyway) Kevin didn't stop to argue. He went over to the touch-line and squatted down to clear his head. Fleetingly, Keith Nash wondered whether to bring on his substitute, but decided against it. He, too, realized that the first half was almost over and during the interval he could discuss the situation with Kevin and discover how United's chief striker felt. As it turned out, however, he didn't have to wait as long as that.

When Ben Fairfield lost the ball in a tackle on the halfway line the United centre-half booted the ball up-field in the hope that somebody would make use of it. The Rangers' right-half went for the ball and tried to control it even before it bounced. In his haste he misjudged things and succeeded only in slicing the ball out towards the wing. It would have run straight into touch for there was no player out there.

Kevin chose that moment to look up. He saw the ball coming straight towards him and he reacted instinctively. He stood up, leapt across the touch-line and ran on to the ball as if it had been passed to him. With no one on hand to challenge him for possession Kevin raced forward. Glancing up, he saw that his centre-forward was moving towards the penalty area and unmarked by any defender. Kevin hit a long pass to him in the same moment that the referee blew furiously on his whistle.

That pass was well-judged. The centre-forward didn't have to change his line by so much as a centimetre as the ball ran across in front of him. He took it with him for one stride before firing an excellent shot into the net. True, the goalkeeper had made no effort to stop it. For Jackie Allerton had been playing to the whistle. So he knew that the goal wouldn't count.

Kevin was furious. He had recovered sufficiently now to show all his old aggression—even when talking to a referee. "Hey, Ref," he protested vehemently, "what was wrong with that? That was a great goal."

"No, it wasn't, sonny," the referee replied mildly. "I stopped the play because you committed an infringement."

"Me!" Kevin exploded. "I didn't do nothing wrong!" His grammar sometimes suffered when he believed he'd been misjudged.

"I'm afraid you did," continued the referee as he awarded a free kick to Rangers. "You were off the field of play and you are not allowed to come back without the referee's permission. You really should read the rules of Association Football, you know, before you become a player."

That silenced Kevin. It was not often that he had to admit to any ignorance on the subject of soccer but that was one rule he hadn't known.

"Never mind," said the referee in very kindly

fashion, "a game's never wasted if you learn something from it. And I'm glad to see that you feel well enough to join in this game again. You have my permission to resume."

Rangers' right-half took the kick and made good use of it for the ball was aimed at Trevor Shipway and it reached him. But, as Trevor brought it under control, the referee's whistle sounded for half-time.

Both teams used the interval to discuss tactics. The Oakland players huddled together on the opposite side of the pitch from United but they still tended to talk in whispers. With so much at stake on the result of this match neither side could afford to give the opposition a clue about how they intended to set about improving their position in the second period.

"You're having a great game, Nick," Trevor said with a grin. Nick just shrugged. "It suits me —and the team," he replied. "So long as United worry about me you'll get the chances to score. So see that you take them."

Trevor wasn't too pleased with that remark and he switched the conversation to talk about how they should hold on to their lead. To Nick, that was a negative approach. One goal was rarely enough in any match and he believed that Rangers should plan how to score again.

Another goal should finish United; but if they were only one down they'd strive for all they were worth to get at least an equalizer.

Right from the kick-off, Bank Vale showed that was their intention. Edward Lancaster was still keeping a wary eye on Nick but his team-mates were chasing into the Oakland half as if they'd been told the net was full of free season tickets for Albion's matches and it was a case of first come, first served. Both Ben Fairfield and Trevor Shipway dropped back to help out in defence. Only Jazz Fagan and Rupert Mitchell were left up-field—apart, of course, from Nick who was still an isolated figure in red on the right touch-line.

With the ball bouncing high and always difficult to control on the hard pitch there were plenty of mistakes as the battle for superiority was waged. Several times United should have had the ball in the net. They were foiled only by mis-kicks on the part of their own attackers or lucky last-ditch clearances by Oakland defenders.

As the minutes ticked away United threw more and more men up into attack but even then they didn't relax their guard on Nick, who had been a spectator for practically the whole of the match. But now his patience was beginning to wear a bit thin; moreover, he wasn't impressed by Rangers' tactics. It really was the wrong policy simply to try and hold on to so slender a lead.

Quite casually, Nick began to wander along the touch-line into his team's half of the field. Then, for a change and also to warm up a bit, he broke into a sprint.

Edward Lancaster followed suit. Nick turned, and chased back in the opposite direction. Edward did likewise. To the handful of spectators round the pitch it looked as though the two boys were engaged in a private relay match. Edward was the first to begin to feel rather foolish. Still, he'd had his orders and he was determined to stick to them, whatever happened.

"If I were a girl, would you follow me into the Ladies'?" Nick asked him with a grin. Edward blushed to the colour of his hair but he didn't reply. The whole situation was bad enough without Nick making stupid jokes.

Their curious behaviour during those few moments had also caught the eye of Phil Astbury,

Rangers' right-back. So, when the ball came to him in a tight situation, he took a desperate measure to clear his lines. He booted the ball as hard as possible in Nick's direction. The slight wind that had blown up during the course of the match helped to carry it right over the halfway line.

Nick made up his mind at once to go for it. Yet he didn't attempt to move at top speed. Already, a plan had formed in his mind.

Edward Lancaster had almost been caught by surprise—but not quite. So when Nick ran, he ran. The ball was dropping as Nick reached it— with Edward no more than half-a-stride behind him. Nick appeared to start to jump, and then change his mind.

For suddenly he ducked his head away and allowed the ball to bounce behind him. And, as it touched the ground, Nick was already spinning round in a half-circle. Ths time Lancaster was caught unawares. He had to brake hurriedly and he slithered past the point where Nick had turned. And now Nick had opened up a gap between them of a few precious metres.

He raced down the wing, pushing the ball well ahead of him. Edward was in pursuit but, even without having a ball to worry about, he was having difficulty in catching up. But now United's centre-half, who had stayed back, was coming across to provide support for Lancaster. Then Nick started to windmill his left arm—and on

the opposite wing Jazz Fagan reacted to the signal. He started to run at speed—and he was cutting inside at the same time.

Only a split-second before the United centre-half reached him Nick, who had been veering slightly leftwards, suddenly belted the ball with all the strength he possessed. It flew over the centre-half's head, across to the other wing. And Jazz, now in top gear, seized it eagerly. Sensibly, his opposing full-back moved across diagonally to try and close off the most direct route into the box.

Jazz, however, had seen that Nick was still tearing in towards goal from the right. The centre-half had been beaten and out-paced but Lancaster was still giving chase. Nick wasn't worried about that. He was confident he could outwit Edward if the need arose. But it didn't.

For Jazz, who had the highest regard for Nick's shooting skills, now returned the compliment of a long pass. The ball zoomed across the pitch again so that to some it seemed as though Jazz and Nick were playing some sort of tennis match. Nick hardly had to slow up at all as the ball bounced in front of him. From just inside the box he smashed the ball on the half-volley—and if there'd been any justice it would have made the net billow.

As it was, the goalkeeper's dive was a good one. He reached the ball almost at full stretch with his hand but he hadn't a hope of holding it. As it skidded clear of his grasp Jazz, who'd never stopped running, swept in and, with the greatest economy of effort, side-footed it into the open goal.

Bank Vale United 0, Oakland Rangers 2.

Edward Lancaster wasn't the only United player who was in despair. It was diabolical. The only time Nick had made a forward move in the whole of the match and he had set up a perfect goal! As a result, United had lost a home match they were so anxious to win.

For the referee signalled the end of the game less than three minutes later and United hadn't managed to pull back even one goal. Rangers were thoroughly elated, their opponents cast in gloom.

What really pleased Nick now was that his old injury hadn't troubled him once during the game. It was true he hadn't done much work until the last few minutes but in the race into the penalty area for the second goal he had exerted himself fully. And there had been no hint of any protest from his thigh muscles.

So now he could concentrate completely on the next two stages of the Superstar Contest to be held during the coming week.

Five

The time of the swimming race had been well chosen: after school finished, but before tea began, on Tuesday. It was a time when the Town Baths were not likely to be in much demand and Trevor Shipway and his fellow judges were hoping that the race would take place without any interference whatsoever from outsiders. Only Nick Abel-Smith was a bit put out: he had been planning to have the whole evening free to visit the fairground.

The Great November Fair was something he looked forward to every year. Best of all were the dodgem cars. He would have as many goes on them as he could afford: and for weeks he had been saving his pocket money.

For the moment, however, he had to concentrate his thoughts on the swimming race. If he was to have any chance at all of winning the captaincy prize it was essential for him to pick up some points by finishing in the first three. He couldn't afford to let Dinger Bell draw further ahead of him.

Little was known about the relative swimming abilities of the contestants, mainly because no two of them went to the same school. Naturally, Dinger had been boasting that he would win easily—but then he claimed that he would be first in every stage of the tournament. According to him, it was a sheer fluke that he hadn't won the sprint.

Nick was one of the last to arrive at the Town Baths because his school was some way from the town centre. Most of the other boys had already changed but Trevor had insisted that none of them should enter the water until the race started. He was determined to see that the conditions should be fair to everyone.

Only a few moments after Nick had chosen his cubicle and started to change there was a tap on the door.

"Hey, Nick, you're wanted," someone said in an urgent whisper. "Trevor wants a quick word with you."

Nick recognized the voice of Mark Haskayne,

Oakland's left-back. He couldn't imagine why Trevor should want to speak to him, for only a couple of minutes earlier he had been telling everyone to hurry up.

Nick paused only to slip his jacket on again but by the time he opened the door Mark had already vanished. He still wasn't in sight when Nick arrived at the side of the pool and asked Trevor what he wanted.

The Rangers' captain was puzzled. "I don't want anything—except for you to hurry up and get changed and get down here. The rest of the lads are practically ready for the race to start. So don't hang about, Nick."

"But you sent Haskayne up to fetch me," Nick pointed out.

Trevor shook his head. "No, I didn't. He must be having a joke or something. So, come on, Nick, hurry up."

Vowing that he would deal with young Haskayne as soon as possible, Nick bounded up the steps and back into his cubicle. It was only when he'd stripped off completely that he discovered his swimming trunks were missing. They'd been wrapped inside his towel and he knew that he couldn't have lost them on the way to the Baths. But where had they gone?

"Nick!" Trevor Shipway was yelling at the top of his voice from the edge of the bath. "We're not going to wait any longer for you. If you aren't down here in ten seconds flat I'm going to start the race. It's in the rules, you know—everyone's got to be ready at the same time. No excuses allowed."

Nick bit his lip. He knew he daren't delay any longer, but, equally, he had to get hold of some swimming trunks. Hastily, he pulled on his underpants and opened the door.

"Anybody got any swimming trunks I can borrow?" he called out. His fellow competitors and the other members of the team stared up at him, astonished. All, that is, except one: Dinger Bell. He was grinning like a Cheshire cat.

"Nobody's got a spare pair," he called with the certainty of someone who'd already checked that point. "So you'll have to swim without them— or withdraw from the race!"

Nick knew now who had pinched his trunks. Mark Haskayne was a pal of Dinger's, so the two of them had fixed up this trick between them.

He wasn't at all surprised to note that Haskayne was nowhere in sight. He had cleared off with the trunks until the race was under way.

"Okay, then, I'm coming," Nick replied. He would simply have to swim in his underpants. There was no alternative, for he had no intention of missing the race.

Trevor gulped, and two of the other boys gave a sort of wolf whistle of surprise, as Nick bounded down the steps and sped round the pool to take his place in the line-up.

"Good job there are no girls here at the moment," Phil Astbury said with a laugh. Nick had been thinking exactly the same thing. What was worrying him was the fact that the elastic round the top of his shorts wasn't very strong. He took the precaution of holding them up as he ran. Once he was in the water he'd just have to hope for the best....

"Right, lads," Trevor intoned in familiar fashion. "You all know the rules. Keep to a straight line. No bumping when you make the turn. This is a free-style race so you can use whatever stroke you like. Three lengths of the bath. Okay? Get set, then. Steady!"

The pistol cracked—and the six swimmers

dived into the water. Stage Two of the Superstar Contest had begun.

It must have seemed inevitable to spectators and competitors alike that Dinger Bell should storm into the lead from the start. Powerfully built with what somebody had described as "a barrel for a chest", the left-half was cleaving through the water like a pilot launch. His breast-stroke was strong and well measured and, of course, he had no lack of faith in his own ability to stay in front. By now Mark Haskayne had re-appeared from his hiding place and was cheering his pal on noisily.

The slightly-built Ben Fairfield was already in last place—swimming steadily enough but making no real progress. It passed through Trevor's mind that Ben had been rather foolish to compete for the captaincy. Although he was a fair soccer player, he lacked personality as well as strength. All the same, Ben had a dogged persistence and he wouldn't give in a second time as he had done in the sprint race. He was going to keep going right to the end this time and his first aim was to overtake Scott Hooston, the swimmer who was now only half-a-length or so ahead of him.

73

Nick had made a flying start and was lying in second position when he realized that something was going wrong below the water-line. He had been employing the fastest stroke of all, the crawl, but he lost his rhythm as he tried to cope with his problem. The trouble, of course, was around his waist—or, rather, a little below that level. For his substitute trunks were now completely saturated and threatening to entangle his legs as they slipped lower and lower.

He struggled to keep control of them but that was hindering his progress in the race. Jazz Fagan was now Dinger's closest rival, with Rupert Mitchell moving very easily in third place, as Nick fell back. He had already lost several lengths by his own estimation and he dare not drop any further back. Even Scott Hooston was catching up with him.

The spectators were beginning to think that the race was all over bar the shouting. Dinger had set up such a good lead that he looked a certainty to win—although one or two boys had noted how well Rupert was swimming. He seemed not to be exerting himself very much at this stage and yet he was keeping level with Jazz.

"Hey, look!" somebody shouted in a voice

that held a mixture of excitement and alarm. "Nick's disappeared!"

It was true. The swimmer who'd been lying in fourth place had suddenly vanished.

"Gosh," Trevor said to his fellow judges. "Do you think he's drowning? We'd better get some help."

"No, hang on," Jackie Allerton replied. He had seen some fairly violent movement under the water—and a moment later Nick's head and shoulders broke the surface.

His return was accompanied by a great deal of spluttering and splashing but apart from that he appeared none the worse for his submerged spell. In fact, although the spectators weren't aware of it, Nick was now feeling better than at any time since the race began. For he had freed himself of the restriction that had threatened to put him out of action completely—his pants. It had been the only thing to do for he couldn't continue with them round his knees.

As most of his body was below the water-line no one could really object to him swimming without any clothes on. And, rather to his own surprise, Nick now experienced a feeling of total freedom. At last he could concentrate totally on winning the race.

Dinger had turned at the end of the first length of the pool and was still way in front. Rupert Mitchell had moved up smoothly into second place as Jazz Fagan lost ground. In third place was Scott Hooston who had changed from the breast-stroke to the crawl and had made excellent progress. Nick was now a couple of lengths ahead of the persevering Ben Fairfield.

By the time the swimmers reached the second, and final, turn the race had really warmed up. Dinger still led but his advantage was being reduced all the time. For, once again, Dinger was running out of steam and Rupert seemed to be gaining momentum with every metre he covered. Mitchell had told no one that at his own school he was a member of the junior swimming team and was regularly chosen to swim the last leg in relay races.

Scott Hooston, too, was swimming exceptionally well now but still not gaining on Rupert. Scott's battle was going to be with Nick who, having overtaken the tiring Jazz Fagan, was in hot pursuit of the three leaders. He had no time to be furious about the trick that had cost him so many lengths; all he could think about was picking up some points in the Superstar Contest. He couldn't afford to finish out of the first three this time.

At the very moment that Rupert Mitchell drew level with Dinger, Nick pulled alongside Scott. And for the remainder of the race the spectators were in a predicament: there were two separate battles going on out in the pool and they wanted to watch both.

Dinger was the first to rally and, momentarily, he regained the lead over Rupert. But Rupert had paced himself well and he knew how much he had in reserve. Scott, however, was really fading now. He began to roll in the water and Nick knew he had the measure of him. It was just a question of choosing the moment to pull ahead. By now he'd realized that he had no hope of catching the two leaders.

Suddenly, Dinger began to lose his rhythm and flounder. This had been the best swim of his life but, once again, he found he had nothing in reserve as the finishing line came almost within reach.

Rupert slid past him as cleanly as a dolphin and Dinger could have wept with frustration.

As it was, he swallowed rather a lot of water. And that really finished him. His only consolation was that he held on to take second place—for the second time in two events.

The race for third place was almost as close. Scott Hooston was no more willing to give in than Dinger had been. Over the last few metres he and Nick were swimming shoulder to shoulder as each strove to gain an advantage over the other. In that all-out effort Scott had somehow managed to recover his stroke, while Nick had perhaps been too confident and had temporarily relaxed.

But, as they stretched forward to touch the tiled wall at the end of their swim, Nick thought he'd just got the verdict. Trevor hesitated a moment before giving the result for it had been a very tight finish—almost a dead-heat.

"Nick Abel-Smith is third," he announced—and Nick allowed his features to relax into a rare grin. Scott didn't seem too pleased at first but he accepted the decision sportingly enough.

Nick was just about to haul himself out of the water when he remembered his predicament. He slid back until the water came up to his waist.

"Hand me a towel, will you, Trevor," he asked. "Any one will do."

"Eh? Why, what's wrong with your own?" Trevor said, puzzled.

"I haven't got any clothes on, that's why," Nick explained patiently. "All my things are up in my cubicle."

"Oh, yes, sure," Trevor said, seizing the nearest towel. It belonged to Dinger Bell but neither Trevor nor Nick was aware of that. In any case, Nick would only have regarded it as some sort of justice. He knew very well that Dinger had organized the theft of his swimming trunks.

At that moment Dinger was thinking more about his success than drying himself. The three points he'd picked up for second place put him into the lead in the Contest, as he was quick to point out to everyone within earshot.

"*Joint* first place, if you don't mind," Rupert Mitchell said importantly. "Don't forget I got a point from the sprint, so I've now got six points, just like you."

"Right, lads, the overall position in the Contest is now as follows," Trevor said with the force of a junior Tannoy system. "Bell and Mitchell six points each; Fagan, five points; Abel-Smith, one point; Hooston and Fairfield, no points each."

While he had their attention—for they'd all been listening in spite of knowing the positions for themselves—he added something for good measure.

"The shooting match was going to be held on Friday night, but that won't be possible now because Mr Allerton's club has had to change the date of a fixture they'd arranged. So instead we're going along there tomorrow night. I'm sorry this is such short notice but we can't do anything about it.

"Still, it means that we won't have long to wait to find out who can shoot straight—and who's going to take an outright lead in the Superstar Contest."

Nick hurried up to his cubicle to dry and get changed. He wasn't at all surprised to find that while he'd been away someone—obviously Haskayne—had returned his swimming trunks. The stupid thief hadn't even had the sense to try and hide them to make it appear as though Nick had misplaced them. They were lying on top of his clothes. Ah well, Nick thought, at least he could now wear them under his trousers ... for his pants were at the bottom of the pool.

A bull-like roar from Dinger signalled the left-half's discovery that someone had gone off with his towel. As he charged up the steps to recover it, Nick hastily rolled the towel into a ball. He stepped out of the cubicle as Dinger raced towards him.

"Sorry I had to borrow your towel, Bell," he called. "Here it is."

And he hurled it as hard as he could. It sailed over Dinger's head, unfolded in flight—and then gently floated down into the pool. Nick turned calmly, went back into his cubicle and locked the door. That had settled his score with Dinger Bell very nicely.

A couple of hours later Nick was still thinking about scores—but of a rather different kind. Immediately after finishing tea, he had set off for the fairground. His mind was full of how he was going to spend his money and how many dodgem rides he could afford. But after only one trip on the Caterpillar and three attempts to win a coconut he had come upon the rifle stalls.

He couldn't help thinking about the shooting match the following evening. For a few minutes he watched some boys firing away at table tennis balls balanced on water spouts and knocking down tiny metal figures cut in the shape of human beings.

There were some prizes to be won for good scores but Nick was interested less in them than in the chance of getting in some useful practice with a rifle. Really, it was an ideal opportunity to prepare for the next event in the Superstar Contest. He wouldn't admit it to anyone but he was rather worried by his failure to pick up more than one point so far. He knew he couldn't afford to do badly on the rifle range.

As soon as a gun was free Nick paid over his money to the stall-holder and was shown how to load the rifle with the small metal pellets shaped rather like mushrooms.

There was very little recoil from the gun when he fired his first shot—but it was enough to surprise him. Where the pellet finished up he had no idea but the metal figure he'd been aiming at hadn't fallen. He knew that he had to knock down eight of the men figures with the ten pellets he'd been given in order to win a prize— so now he could afford only one more miss. His second shot brought no better result. But he thought he'd missed by only a narrow margin.

Nick took a more careful aim this time—and actually saw the bullet bounce off the target. It came back almost straight at him and Nick naturally tried to duck out of the way. By now the stallholder had no other customers to deal with and he could give his whole attention to this young would-be marksman.

As if determined to help a customer to walk off with one of his prizes, he came round to the front of the stall and demonstrated how the stock of the rifle should be pulled into the shoulder. He explained how the touch on the trigger should be very light and how to "squeeze it gently. Don't snatch at it. You'll miss by a mile if you tug at it like you were doing."

Nick thought that was a bit unfair for he had managed to hit the target with his third shot. But he knew he was getting good advice so he followed the man's instructions. And he was rewarded with the sight of his first figure keeling over smartly as he fired again.

"That's it, boyo," the stallholder said enthusiastically. "We'll make a top shooter out of you yet."

Nick managed three more "drops" (as the man called them) with his remaining ammunition. So he didn't need any persuading to pay out another 10p for ten more pellets.

"Now you're really getting your eye in," he was told encouragingly as this time he "dropped" seven of the figures. "You don't actually get a prize for that but you deserve one for learning so fast. So there you are, son."

He handed over a smart yellow ballpoint pen which Nick promptly pocketed. He could have bought it in any shop for half the price of the ammunition but that didn't matter.

When Nick checked his financial position he

discovered he'd spent so much at the rifle stall that he could now have only two rides on the dodgems.

Still, the rest of his money had been well spent. So he would just have to make the most of the two rides—and set up a personal record of bumpings on the other cars on the circuit.

He could, for instance, imagine that the car he bumped most frequently was being driven by Dinger Bell.

Six

Jackie Allerton's father had no objection at all to the idea of the boys holding a mini-competition during their visit to the rifle club's range. He seemed to think it showed how enthusiastic they were, although he was rather surprised that only six of them were actually going to take part. The other half-dozen who'd come along were content simply to be spectators. The team's captain, however, had volunteered to act as scorer and was at least as keen about the whole thing as the competitors.

But before he allowed the shooting to start Mr Allerton pointed out some of the dangers of playing about with .22 rifles and said that they should never—*never*—be fired out-of-doors or pointed at anyone "even when you know they're not loaded. Guns like these are *only* to be used on a proper rifle range. Shooting is for sport, not killing birds or animals or people."

His audience listened patiently and promised they would always remember what he'd said. All the same, they could hardly wait for the action to begin. A draw to determine the order of firing had been made before they arrived at the range and, as luck would have it, Dinger Bell's name had come out first. "And that's where I'll finish," he'd been boasting. "I'll give you all a target to aim at but you won't beat my score. I'll hit the bull every time, you'll see."

Nick was to shoot fourth and, after his practice the previous evening, was confident of getting a good total.

The targets, set up some twenty metres away at the far end of the range, were not as colourful as the boys had expected. They were black in the centre and white elsewhere. The points system, too, was a bit baffling with the black rings counting between 10 and 7 and the white ones between 6 and 4 but nothing below that.

Dinger was, characteristically, impatient to start shooting but he and his rivals had to listen first to another lecture from Mr Allerton on the way to hold the rifle and how to use the sight.

Like the stallholder at the fairground, he wanted the boys to "squeeze the trigger gently and not snatch at it."

That advice was ignored by the impetuous Dinger. He'd no sooner taken aim than he was firing. He seemed to think that he could rival a Western sheriff in the speed of his shooting. It was his bad luck that Mr Allerton decided he might as well let the lad carry on as he was doing so that, when he'd finished, he could point out the folly of not taking your time over your shots.

Each competitor was allowed five shots only— so that the competition wouldn't last too long— and Dinger had been predicting that, of course, he'd get a total of between 45 and 50, the maximum. In fact, when his target was pulled forward on two wire ropes by turning a handle near the firing position it was seen that he had managed to get only one shot in the black part. His score was only 17.

"Now that's what comes of rushing it," Mr Allerton pointed out. "If this boy had taken his time he'd've done a lot better."

Dinger was unwise enough to mutter something about his rifle "not firing straight" but Mr Allerton wasn't going to let that allegation stand.

Every rifle in the Club, he pointed out very firmly, was checked for its accuracy after every session. The weapon that Dinger had been firing was as perfect as all the others.

Ben Fairfield went next and spent almost a minute over every shot. One or two of the boys started to urge him to hurry up but Mr Allerton said it was quite permissible to take five minutes to get off five shots. There was nothing to be gained by treating a rifle like a machine-gun.

But, for all his care, Ben fared little better than Dinger. Only four of his shots had hit the target and his total score was 20. The four marksmen who were left now had every reason to believe that between them they would provide the first three in the competition. It was just a case of which of them would be fourth and not collect any points.

It soon became obvious that Jazz Fagan knew how to fire a rifle. He approached the whole business very coolly, settling himself into a comfortable position and cradling the rifle as though he'd been shooting guns all his life. Only one shot was outside the black rings and even that brought him a 6. When his marks were totted up he had every reason to smile broadly: he had scored 40. Once again, his team-mates began to wonder what Jazz would be like as captain of Oakland Rangers.

Nick had been feeling fairly confident of getting a good score until Jazz completed his five shots. He desperately needed to win an event and he'd been hoping that this was going to be the one. Some of his team-mates, he guessed, were already writing him off as their future captain. He had to prove them wrong.

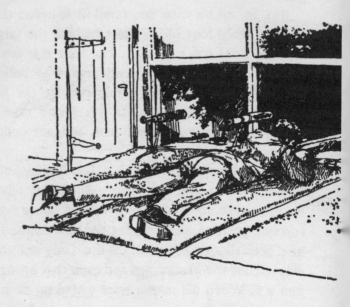

The rifle seemed almost identical with the one he'd been using at the fairground and that made him feel a bit better. With a little help from Mr Allerton he settled himself into the firing position and took careful aim at the target. It was a lot further away than the little metal figures he'd shot at the previous evening. On the other hand, it was bigger.

Very, very gently Nick squeezed the trigger— and the bullet punched a hole through the very

edge of the target.

Nick's mistake shook him. One more failure like that could easily cost him the captaincy. He was mad with himself for not concentrating more; all the same, he had to be calm if he was to make up for it. His second shot brought him his first score: 6. That helped to restore some confidence —and after that he was never out of "the black". Another 25, including a bull, gave him a total of 31. He hadn't beaten Jazz's score but he was well ahead of the others who'd had their turn. With a bit of luck, he would finish second in the competition and pick up three points.

Those hopes were soon dashed. For this was the moment Scott Hooston had been waiting for all day—and even longer. Scott possessed an air rifle of his own and had been firing at targets ever since the previous Christmas when he received the rifle as a present from his uncle.

He'd been delighted when Jackie Allerton had suggested to his fellow judges that rifle shooting should be one of the events in the tournament. It had been difficult to conceal his joy but he had told no one of his hobby. He had simply put in even more practice in the evenings. Now, at last, he was going to make up for all his misfortunes in the sprint and the swimming race.

Mr Allerton noticed at once that Scott was familiar with a rifle. So he expected a good score —and he got one. Scott added a professional touch by examining the rifle very closely and appearing to weigh it in his hands. He took more time than anyone in making himself comfortable in the firing position.

His first shot smacked into the bull, bringing him 10 marks, and his second almost went through the same hole. So, with three bullets left, he'd already drawn ahead of Dinger Bell—something that gave him a lot of satisfaction. Trying, perhaps, a little too hard with his third shot he managed to hit only the "8" ring. But he was back on form with his next shot which punctured the bull again. All he needed to do now, to take the lead from Jazz, was to hit the target inside any of the rings. In fact, he finished with a flourish by scoring 9 for a grand total of 47.

"Good shooting, son," Mr Allerton said warmly to Scott, who was trying not to look too smug. "If you can shoot like that all the time you ought to be a member of my Club. We can do with some good young talent."

He was so pleased that he almost forgot that

93

there was still one boy waiting for his turn on the range. Rupert Mitchell, however, wasn't going to allow anyone to overlook him and he made a fuss about winding in a new target and then settling himself into the firing position.

But it was all in vain for he couldn't match any of the leading scores. He had been too keen to maintain his lead in the Contest and shot both wildly and hastily. Had he taken his time he'd surely have done better, for he hit the bull once and finished with a total of 24.

Mr Allerton was very hospitable and provided the boys with glasses of lemonade and biscuits and invited them to come again; but most of them were rather restless by now. They wanted to get away to discuss the latest stage of the Superstar Contest. It had captured the imagination of all of them—even those who weren't competing for the captaincy—and they were eager to get on with the next competition. The intervals in between the events were getting shorter and shorter—but that was the way they wanted it.

"Right, lads," Trevor began in his customary manner as soon as they were all gathered together around him after leaving the range, "I can now give you the latest up-to-date situation in the

Contest. The total points for each candidate are as follows: Fagan, 8; Bell and Mitchell, 6 each; Hooston, 5; Abel-Smith, 2; Fairfield, nil."

Nick was perhaps the saddest of all of them. He knew that it was still possible for him to win but the shooting match had not helped him to make up any lost ground on the leaders. Indeed, before visiting the range he had been only five points behind Bell and Mitchell; now he was six behind Jazz Fagan. It was true that he had moved just a little closer to Dinger Bell (four points separated them now) but he had set his heart not only on beating Dinger but on becoming the captain of Oakland Rangers. At this moment, that ambition was a long way from being fulfilled.

"Well, the suspense is really building up now, lads," Trevor said, and no one could possibly have argued with him about that statement. "So we don't want to keep everybody waiting for the next competition. The judges have decided that the quarry climb should be held on Saturday morning and not next week as we'd first decided. Right, then, you'd better all get yourselves some good gear to climb in. And we'll all assemble at Cricket Hill Quarry at 10 o'clock on Saturday morning."

"And I hope somebody remembers to bring a stretcher and a first aid box in case anyone falls when they're halfway to the top," Phil Astbury murmured grimly. But no one was listening to him.

Seven

Milder weather had followed the hard frost but by Saturday morning it had turned to rain. Nick was dismayed. He realized that rain could make climbing conditions treacherous; they might even be so bad that the race up the quarry face would have to be postponed. It was hardly an easy climb at the best of times.

The old quarry, abandoned long ago, was halfway up Cricket Hill on the outskirts of the town. As he rode out there on the bus Nick tried to imagine who among his rivals was likely to be the best climber. So far as he knew, none of them had much experience of scaling rock faces or even high walls.

He supposed that the taller boys, such as Scott Hooston and Rupert Mitchell, would have an advantage simply because of their reach. Strength in the arms should count a lot and therefore he

97

was glad he did press-ups every day. Nick knew he was at least as fit as any of his team-mates—and quite probably the fittest of them all.

He wasn't the first to arrive at the quarry. Appropriately, Trevor and his fellow judges were already there and just about to complete the draw for places. Trevor gave him a brief wave and then pulled a scrap of paper out of the school cap they were using.

"Fagan," he said to Jackie Allerton, who dutifully noted the name on a page of his notebook. Then he turned to Nick. "That means you go last," he grinned. "At least you'll know how everybody else has got on by the time it's your turn."

Nick nodded. "Who's first?" he wanted to know.

"Ben Fairfield," Trevor replied. "Then Scott, then Dinger, then Rupert, then Jazz—and then you. Should be a great race. I've borrowed a real stopwatch so we'll be able to time everybody to the split-second. You never know, it could be as close as that."

The rain was still bucketing down and Nick wished they'd get on with it. He took what shelter he could in an old workman's hut which had only two walls still standing and a leaking roof (or what remained of the roof). From where he stood, the face of the quarry looked to be a formidable obstacle. He wasn't sure how high it was—higher than a house, anyway—and few ledges were visible. It would be a case of using whatever finger and toe-holds one could find.

"Jazz Fagan's not here yet but I think we should start without him," Trevor told the assembled members of Oakland Rangers. "He goes next to last, anyway. We said 10 o'clock for the starting time, so we should stick to it."

"Hear, hear!" Dinger called. What he meant was that, as he was present, nothing else mattered. After failing to take any points from the previous event he was determined to regain the lead from Jazz, so if Jazz didn't turn up, well, too bad.

Trevor made a great thing of explaining to Ben Fairfield, the first climber, that he was only to start on a given signal and that the stopwatch would be started simultaneously.

He could take as long as he wanted over the climb but every minute counted, however many times he paused for breath or to find a new hold. If no one actually reached the summit, the winner

would be the one who climbed the highest in the fastest time.

"Ready, Ben?" he asked, and Ben nodded. Trevor had his stopwatch in one hand and his starting pistol in the other—and when he fired the gun Ben sprinted away from the chosen starting line and launched himself at the rock face.

The Rangers inside-left was small but of a compact build. Like Nick, he had strong shoulders and arms but his greatest asset was his sense of balance. He was particularly good at controlling a football in tight situations. For the climb he had dressed in a gaberdine wind-cheater and had wound a thin nylon rope round his waist. He gave the impression that he knew exactly what he was doing.

Ben seemed to have no trouble at all in ascending the quarry wall. He found the best holds with very little hesitation and swung easily up to the next. Just once he dislodged some tiny loose stones, which cascaded into the quarry quite spectacularly, but that didn't bother him. He made no effort to use his rope—because he was doing very well without it.

"Hey, he's going up there just like a monkey.

No problems at all," Jackie Allerton remarked in tones of admiration.

"Must be dead easy, that's why," Dinger Bell retorted. "I'll do it in half the time, you watch."

By now the rain had eased off considerably, for which several of the climbers were thankful. Apart from Dinger, they were aware that Ben was setting them a tough target.

The pacesetter was now within a few metres of the summit. Not once had he looked down. Now, for the first time, he paused as he searched for the easiest route on to the grassy slope that marked the top of the quarry. Then, as he scrambled on to it, he stood up and waved his arms excitedly. He had completed his climb.

"Four minutes and 13 seconds," Trevor announced. "Pretty good, that, I reckon. Whoever beats it deserves to win."

Ben was given the thumbs-up signal and he now made his way up the slope and over the guard fence to return to the bottom of the quarry by an easier route.

"Okay, Scott, it's your turn," Trevor said— and then the starting pistol cracked again.

After winning the shooting competition Scott felt that his bad luck was over and that he now had an excellent chance of gaining the coveted prize of the captaincy. He believed that his height would be an advantage in the climb. In common with the majority of his rivals, he was wearing his soccer tracksuit and plimsolls.

He, too, made a good start and actually matched Ben's time to the halfway stage. But then he had difficulty in picking the right holds. First he stretched too far and became unbalanced. Then he could find holds for his fingers but not his feet. Luckily, he was cool enough to think of going back a short way and looking for another route.

He seemed to have one bad moment, just below the summit, but when he completed his climb in 5min. 28sec. he, too, had given the impression that it was a fairly easy accomplishment.

Dinger shot away from the starting line with the intention of demonstrating all his strength and power as he broke the record for the ascent. He tried a spectacular leap and grabbed at a jutting rock to haul himself up the first few metres. As he did so heavy rain began to fall again. He would claim afterwards that he'd been blinded by it but the truth was that he had neglected care for sheer speed.

For he had reached a height of only about four metres when his foot slipped. His fingers clawed for a firm hold as he felt himself falling. For a moment or two he seemed to hang in mid-air—and then he crashed back to the ground and landed in a heap.

The three judges were the first to reach him. Dinger tried to get to his feet but the pain in his right knee was bad enough for him to sink back on to the ground.

"Have you bust anything?" Trevor inquired anxiously. Already he was thinking about his team's match the following day with Merrywood Colts, the League leaders. It would be a bad blow to Rangers if Dinger had to drop out with an injury.

"Don't think so," Dinger muttered. "But I think I've twisted it. It hurts a lot."

"You tried to go too fast," Ben said. He could afford to be sympathetic but he was really speaking from experience.

"See if you can walk all right," Trevor advised, helping Dinger to his feet. "It's no good letting an injury like this seize-up."

Dinger wasn't too happy about that idea but he didn't want to give the impression that he was

104

just making an excuse for his climbing errors. Shrugging aside the support offered by his pals, Dinger hobbled around for a bit, wincing with almost every step. He tried to flex his knee but that really was painful. Eventually he accepted a helping hand and made for the shelter of the hut where he sat down on an old wooden box.

"Er, you're dropping out of the climb now, are you, Dinger?" Trevor inquired with a rather unfortunate choice of words.

"I might have a go a bit later on when I feel better," the injured left-half replied.

"I'm afraid that's not permitted in the rules," Trevor told him. "Actually, I haven't stopped the watch yet. So you've already had 12 minutes and 38—no, 39—seconds. You've had it as far as the first two places are concerned and I expect the next climber will get up there in less time than you've taken so far."

Dinger started to jump up in protest but the pain in his knee forced him to sit down again hurriedly. He contented himself with muttering something about the rules being rotten and unfair before conceding that he'd have to withdraw from this event.

Rupert Mitchell, the next to climb, was in a

quandary. He was hoping to gain the overall lead in the tournament after failing with the rifle but Dinger's misfortune was a warning not to rush things. He didn't want to lose his place in the football team but he had to do a fast climb to overtake Scott and Ben.

Once again, the rain had begun to ease off. Rupert made a cautious start but he gained confidence as steadily as he gained height. Then, just when he seemed to be going really well, he suffered the same sort of problems as Scott had done. The best holds were in the wrong places for a boy as tall as Rupert. He hated the idea of going back even a few centimetres and so he wasted valuable time as he sought different ledges for his hands and feet.

When he did get going again he tried to make up the lost time, stretched too far, slipped precariously—and caused plenty of hearts to beat a lot faster among the watchers below. That incident put a brake on Rupert's progress. And so when, greatly to his own relief, he reached the top the time he had taken was 9min. 17sec.—more than twice that recorded by Ben Fairfield.

Although conscious of his position as tournament leader, Jazz Fagan was determined to take no chances. He was well aware that he couldn't now be overtaken by anyone until the next, and final, event was decided. So he would be quite happy to pick up just one point. To everyone's surprise he had arrived equipped with a crash helmet which he strapped on before he started his climb. Since Dinger's fall none of the boys had accused him of being soft; they knew the helmet made sense.

Jazz's ascent was totally unspectacular. Not once did he seem to be in trouble and he kept up a regular rhythm of pause, go, pause. No one had any doubt the whole way that he would reach the top. The time he took was 6min. 40sec. So, for the present, he had achieved his objective: third place.

Nick was thinking that his luck had begun to change. The rain had stopped and he knew that unless he made a really bad mistake during his climb he should collect some points in his bid for the captaincy. Physically, he and Ben were very similar and Nick's sense of balance was at least as good as his rival's. Moreover, he had watched very, very carefully when Ben was climbing. He was going to take exactly the same route.

Right from the start, Nick was surprised at how

easy the climb was. Ledges and crannies for fingers and toes were plentiful, though most of them hadn't been visible from the floor of the quarry. He had time to think that Dinger Bell had been stupid to try and gallop his way to the top. He was wearing his own watch and so he kept a check of the time. At the halfway stage, he could tell that he was keeping pace with Ben. So ... just a little more effort....

Nick was more astonished than afraid when his foot suddenly slipped and he felt himself beginning to slither backwards. What he had thought was solid stone had turned out to be loose earth and it had crumbled away under his weight. The spectators caught their breath again as they watched him struggle to retain his hold on the rock face.

It was his ability to keep his balance in an awkward situation that saved him from disaster. For a moment or two all his weight was on his left leg—and then he swung himself across to the right to reach a ledge which, thankfully, was quite wide. Nick discovered that the incident had made him sweat a bit but his nerve wasn't affected. He simply steadied himself, worked out a new route and then resumed his climb.

When he reached the summit he immediately checked his watch. According to his calculations he had taken 4min. 43secs. In fact, Trevor had timed it at two seconds shorter, though that made no difference at all to the result of the climbing competition. Ben was the clear winner, Nick was second and Scott third.

With his usual sense of timing Trevor had waited until Nick rejoined them before confirming the new points totals: Fagan, 8; Bell, Hooston and Mitchell, 6 each; Abel-Smith and Fairfield, 5 each. By then even the slowest thinkers among them had worked out what the totals meant: that any one of the candidates could still win the first and only prize—the captaincy of Oakland Rangers!

Dinger Bell had gone one better and worked out a more unlikely situation. "If Jazz comes second in the penalty kick competition and I win it—or Mitchell or Hooston—then it'll be a dead-heat between us!"

That thought left them all speechless for a moment or two as they began to wonder how a problem like that could be sorted out.

"Well, we'll just have to hope that doesn't happen," Trevor said without intending to insult any of the candidates concerned. None of them, however, was listening to him. They were all thinking about their own personal techniques for taking penalty kicks.

"I think we'd better hold the final competition straight after tomorrow's match," Trevor went on after having a word with his fellow judges. Then he noticed Dinger Bell, who was still sitting on the old box. "That is, so long as everyone's fit to take his five penalty kicks. And we won't want any injuries during the match, either."

He paused—and then added: "But it's a vital match, this one with Merrywood. We've got to knock them off the top of the League. That's more important than anything else, lads. So you've all got to give everything you've got and not be thinking all the time about who's going to be the next captain of Rangers."

Eight

At half-time the top-of-the-table clash between Rangers and Merrywood Colts was still goal-less. In spite of the fact that they were away from home, Merrywood were playing anything but a defensive game. They had reached the top of the League by concentrating on attack and they saw no reason to change their tactics simply because Rangers were their closest challengers. Their captain was their centre-forward, Gordon Hammond, and so far this season he had scored in every match. He didn't intend his record to end against Oakland; indeed, he had promised himself a hat trick.

The player who had so far denied him even one goal was Jackie Allerton. He was having a positively inspired game and two of his saves, one from a downward header, the other from a fiercely hit drive from almost point-blank range, were almost in the miraculous class. Gordon, to his credit, had actually congratulated the Rangers' goalkeeper—and then wandered back upfield, shaking his head in disbelief. Jackie wasn't the only barrier to Merrywood's progress, however; both Rangers' full-backs were in exceptional form and, playing just in front of them, Dinger Bell was also having a superb game.

Dinger seemed to have thrown off the effects of his fall the previous day although he'd taken the precaution of wearing a bandage on his injured knee. One or two of the Merrywood forwards had assumed that the bandage indicated a weakness; the almost ferocious tackles they'd been subjected to by the Rangers' left-half had soon changed their minds.

In every game he played, Dinger never gave less than all he possessed in enthusiasm, spirit, strength and skill.

Nick was seeing almost as little of the ball as he had done in the game against Bank Vale United. Both Ben Fairfield and, to a lesser extent, Trevor Shipway had dropped back to forage in midfield and neither was having much success in winning possession. The only real shot that Rangers had managed was from Nick—a swerving effort from just inside the box that hadn't caused much trouble to Merrywood's goalkeeper.

"We must attack more in the second half," Trevor said during the interval. No one was going to dispute that; the problem was how to do it when Merrywood were dominating the game through the strength of their own forwards and midfield players.

"I think you should bring on Scott Hooston as the substitute," Nick commented. "We could do with his height in midfield at the moment."

"I was just thinking of that," Trevor replied, and he was being quite truthful. "Ben, I think you could do with a break. Scott, you can take his place."

Nick was impressed. He could think of other captains who would have resisted that idea just because someone else had mentioned it first. Rangers, he had to acknowledge, had been very fortunate in having Trevor to lead them. Nick hoped that he himself would do as well when he took over from Shipway. For he had no doubt at all now that he was going to win the Superstar Contest.

It was that confidence that allowed him now to devote all his thoughts to winning the game against

Merrywood. For nothing less than victory would be acceptable, especially as Rangers were the home side. As the referee signalled to the teams to take up their positions again Nick had a quick word with Trevor. He had worked out a plan that could win the match....

Merrywood resumed exactly where they had left off—on the attack. Carl Beckingham was being given a torrid time by Gordon Hammond but not once had he committed a foul against the centre-forward. So it surprised Gordon as much as anyone else when Carl suddenly grabbed his opponent round the waist to prevent him getting clean away with the goal practically at his mercy.

Carl got a stern lecture from the referee on the subject of "professional" fouls—and Merrywood were awarded a free kick only just outside the box. From that kick Gordon himself tried to blast a hole in the Rangers' defensive wall and when the ball did somehow get through Jackie Allerton brought off another flying save with one hand. It was that save that helped Oakland to begin to believe that this was going to be their day after all—that all the luck was on their side.

Yet all the pressure was still coming from

Merrywood. Time and again their blue-shirted attackers swarmed round the Rangers' goal, only for a Rangers' defender (or, more likely, their invincible goalkeeper) to thwart them. Meanwhile, Scott Hooston was having a good game in his unaccustomed position in midfield.

Trevor had every reason to congratulate himself on his decision to make the substitution. He himself was still hoping for a breakaway from which Rangers would get a scoring chance. He knew that this game was going to be decided by a single goal—and that goal had to come from Oakland. So he hovered around the halfway line, waiting for the ball to come his way.

The match had only seven minutes to run when the ball did, at last, reach Trevor. He had almost given up hope of getting a chance of scoring the winner. But now that it was here he wasn't going to waste it. Gathering the ball, he raced through the middle—and Nick ran with him.

The Colts' defence hadn't made the mistake of straying upfield in support of their forwards; they were too well disciplined for that. Their centre-half moved in to challenge Trevor for possession but was beaten by sheer speed. But Trevor didn't try to take on the whole defence on his own;

when the next opponent loomed up he slid the ball into Nick's path—and kept running for the return pass.

Trevor was right on the edge of the penalty area when the ball was returned to him; and in that moment his legs were swept from under him by a tackle that was over-exuberant rather than criminal. The referee, however, had no hesitation in blowing up for a foul. Nick dashed across to Trevor and helped him to his feet; and as he did so he explained rapidly that this was the moment to put his plan into action. He had already warned Scott and Jazz and Rupert what to expect—and what parts they were to play. Trevor nodded his agreement.

Now, as the Merrywood defenders built their own wall of defence, Nick wandered away to his left. Jazz was sauntering in from his wing with the air of a player only marginally interested in what was going to happen and not expecting to be involved in it. With equal casualness, Scott drifted in the opposite direction as his captain and Rupert Mitchell huddled over the ball.

The referee's arm was raised, indicating an indirect free kick, and his whistle shrilled. Ignoring Rupert on his right, Trevor hit the ball hard to his left—straight towards Nick. That was what the Colts had expected: Nick was the obvious target because the accuracy of his shooting was almost a legend in the League.

But Nick confounded them completely by jumping over the ball and allowing it to run

through to Jazz, who was no longer the mere spectator he'd appeared to be.

The defenders who'd rushed out towards Nick now paused—and that was fatal. For Jazz had flicked the ball to his left, turned and, with his left foot, swung a beautifully judged centre towards the far post. Rushing in to meet it was Scott Hooston. By now the defenders were in utter confusion, not knowing who to mark. It hadn't occurred to them to move out of the danger zone to place the Rangers' forwards offside.

Scott jumped to meet the ball: he flicked it downwards and sideways exactly as he'd been told to do. Unlike his opponents, Nick knew what was happening—and he pounced. Darting forward, he reached the ball on the half-volley and forced it over the line with the sole of his left boot.

"Great goal, great goal!" Trevor roared as he flung his arms round the scorer. "That was the greatest free kick anyone's ever seen!"

He had every right to take some of the credit for his own part in the movement but he was also acknowledging that everyone involved in it had reacted perfectly. But the real skill had come from Nick in devising the ploy; it had been a stroke of genius to use a decoy and then a double switch of direction.

Merrywood knew then that the tide had turned against them but they didn't allow themselves to drown in their sorrow. For the remaining minutes of the match they drove forward again and again —but all to no avail. When the final whistle blew they had lost not only the match but the leadership of the Sunday Junior League. Rangers had succeeded them by a single point.

"We'll get our revenge in the return game," Gordon Hammond promised as he walked towards the changing-rooms. And then he realized that only his own players were listening to him. The Rangers' team and their supporters were all crowding round one of the goals. They seemed to have forgotten the match that had just ended. Puzzled, Gordon went over to see what was happening, and someone told him about the Superstar Contest and the final event that was about to take place: the penalty kick competition.

For what seemed like the umpteenth time since the idea of the Contest was launched everyone concerned was listening attentively to Trevor Shipway. He knew that this was going to be one of his last duties as captain and he was making the most of it. Each player, he announced, would be allowed five kicks but he had to score first time, not from any rebound. If there was a tie for first place when all the kicks had been taken the boys involved would continue taking kicks in turn until one failed to score.

Jackie Allerton had agreed to be the goalkeeper for the entire competition because he thought it might be unfair if there was a change at any stage. And, as Trevor emphasized, the important thing was that the contest should be fair to everyone all the time—as it certainly had been so far. The draw order was: Ben, Dinger, Rupert, Nick, Scott and Jazz.

By a strange coincidence Ben had been first into action in the previous event, and second the time before that. Somehow it didn't seem to him to be a happy omen, even though he had won the climbing race. He had to set a target again— and shooting had never been his greatest asset. For one thing, he didn't possess a very strong kick. Moreover, he had been out of the afternoon's game since half-time and was feeling a bit chilled.

Every eye was watching him as he stepped back for the first kick of the contest. He tried to put everything he had into it but the ball simply rose gently into Jackie's waiting arms.

Ben's next shot skidded along the ground and Jackie nonchalantly stepped off his line and kicked it back to him. After that, Ben lost heart and so had no hope of getting the ball into the net.

Dinger, however, was full of self-confidence. He had a really powerful shot and his damaged knee wasn't going to inhibit him from using all his strength. He took an astonishingly long run and the ball fairly whistled into the top of the net. Jackie bit his lip and moved a few centimetres along his line in anticipation of the direction of the next cannonball from Dinger. His judgment was good because Dinger's second shot almost followed the first and Jackie got his fingertips to it. But the ball still entered the net. Dinger looked very pleased with himself.

But the smile vanished with the next shot. For, in his eagerness, he misjudged the length of his run. Yet instead of stopping and going back he lunged at the ball—and it flew wide of the right-hand post. Nick, watching as keenly as anyone, closed his eyes briefly in relief.

Dinger thundered in for his fourth shot and this time hit it right—and the net rose like a wind-tossed clothes-line. His final kick brought him his fourth goal in a slightly lucky fashion for the ball went into the net off an upright. Dinger didn't mind how it got there: all he cared about was the fact that to beat him any other candidate now had to score a maximum.

Rupert threatened to do it when he scored with each of his first two shots. But Jackie saved the next two fairly comfortably before Rupert recovered his aim to slip the last shot past him by a very narrow margin.

As Nick stepped forward to place the ball for his first shot the interest of everyone quickened. Nick was renowned as the penalty king for no one could remember hearing of him missing more than one in his entire career. By failing once Dinger had left a chink in his armour.

Nick never took a long run; with him placing, not power, was the important factor. And he placed his first shot just inside Jackie's left-hand post. One problem for Nick was that Jackie had seen him take so many penalties. So he would have a good idea of Nick's favourite spot. He guessed that Nick would try the same shot again —and he was right. The ball went in, but it was a close thing.

Now Nick took even longer over his next shot; taking penalties was something of a war of nerves between kicker and goalie. Jackie was indeed looking anxious, not least because he'd been beaten nine times already. His average was rapidly going down. But he was beaten again when, to everyone's surprise, Nick this time really lashed the ball and it went high over Jackie's head into the top of the net. The shot was so good that it brought spontaneous applause from several spectators.

For his fourth attempt Nick reverted to a low-level shot and the ball hardly rose above the turf as it whizzed into the net well wide of Jackie's diving body.

Nick was now on the threshold of success. One more goal and the captaincy would surely be his. In a sense, he had a free kick. For even if he missed, he and Dinger would be level. Nick couldn't believe that either Scott or Jazz would hit five out of five. What he had forgotten for the moment was that Jazz could still win the Superstar Contest if he finished in second place in this event.

For once, Nick was a trifle too casual. His fifth shot was well hit—but not quite well enough. For, with a mighty leap to his left, Jackie reached the ball and pulled it down before falling on it. By any standards, it was a superlative save.

Until that moment, the prize of the captaincy had seemed to be in Nick's firmest grasp. Nick himself screwed up his eyes and put his hands to his head. One or two boys murmured sympathetic remarks but he didn't really hear them.

But not too astonished to accept—and he and Nick shook hands warmly.

"Right, lads," Nick added. "Well, Trevor's led Rangers to the top of the League. So the best farewell present we can give him is to make sure we stay there—and win the Championship."